THE BIKER'S FORBIDDEN LOVE

UNDERGROUND CROWS MC BOOK FIVE

SADIE KING

LET'S BE BESTIES!

A few times a month I send out an email with new releases, special deals and sneak peeks of what I'm working on. If you want to get on the list I'd love to meet you!

You'll even get a free short and steamy romance when you join.

Sign up here:
www.authorsadieking.com/free

THE BIKER'S FORBIDDEN LOVE
UNDERGROUND CROWS MC

She's my best friend's daughter, totally off limits, and totally irresistible...

I've spent the last three years trying to resist Lily.

She's half my age and the MC president's daughter.

When he asks me to protect her, I do more than that.

I give her my life, my everything.

But what will happen when my best friend finds out what I've been up to with his daughter?

The Biker's Forbidden Love is a best friend's daughter, age gap romance featuring an OTT obsessed biker and the curvy, innocent woman he claims as his own.

Copyright © 2023 by Sadie King.

All rights reserved.

No part of this book may be reproduced in any form or by any electronic or mechanical means, including information storage and retrieval systems, without written permission from the author, except for the use of brief quotations in a book review.

Cover designed by Designrans.

This is a work of fiction. Any resemblance to actual events, companies, locales or persons living or dead, are entirely coincidental.

Please respect the author's hard work and do the right thing.

www.authorsadieking.com

PROLOGUE

Jesse

My bike rumbles down the suburban street, passing perfectly cut hedges and pristine lawns. Heads turn to watch as I cruise past and I give a friendly wave, ignoring the disapproving glances.

The street that Valerie lives on is lined with two-story houses with white picket fences set back on lush green lawns. Until I get to Valerie's house.

Valerie is the lawyer for the Underground Crows MC, and she's also the sister of our club president, Bruno. While her house is as suburban looking as the others, there's thumping bass music coming from the backyard, the sound of chatter, and the smell of barbeque mixed with something suspiciously sweet wafting on the air.

I bet she's as thrilled to be hosting her niece's eighteenth birthday party as I am to be here.

The street in front of her house is crammed with beat-up old cars, the kind that teenagers drive, meaning I have to park a ways down the street. In my saddle bag is a present wrapped in Hello Kitty paper and tied with a pink bow. I don't know if the birthday girl still likes Hello Kitty. I've barely seen her for the last three years since her father, Bruno's, been inside. By the sound of the music and smell of weed, I'm starting to think maybe she doesn't.

I got back to the Sunset Coast yesterday after eight months on the road, and the first thing I did was visit Bruno. That's how I got roped into this.

The last place I want to be is at the eighteenth birthday party of the Pres's daughter. I'd rather be at the clubhouse catching up with my MC brothers and getting shitfaced. But when the President asks you to do something, you do it. Especially when his daughter, Lily, is involved.

Dragging my feet up the stairs, the door opens before I can ring the bell. I'm expecting to see Valerie, but this young woman certainly isn't Valerie. She's wearing tight black jeans and a billowy emerald top that's the exact same shade as her eyes. Her auburn hair is cut shoulder length and dyed black at the tips. She's wearing too much eye makeup, and her lips have a high, glossy shine. One hand rest on her hip and the other hangs by her side, bracelets jangling.

This is definitely not a girl who's still into Hello Kitty.

"Lily?"

She looks like Lily but a grown-up badass version of her.

"What's the matter, Jesse? You look like you've seen a ghost."

"You're all grown up."

It's a stupid thing to say, but this woman's left me speechless.

She smiles at me, and I'm pleased to see there's still softness around her mouth. Lily was always a smiling, happy girl, and I'm not sure I like this tough version of her. Although I can't get my eyes off her tightly pressed together cleavage and the way her jeans hug her voluptuous curves.

The last time I saw Lily she had braces and was gangly and awkward. Now she's all curvy woman and confidence.

I hand the present over, pretty sure she's not going to want the sparkly Hello Kitty purse inside.

"Happy birthday," I mutter. "I don't know what teenage girls are into."

"You shouldn't have."

She stands up on tiptoe and gives me a peck on the cheek. It's meant to be friendly, as a thank you for the present. But as she leans in, I get a whiff of her floral body wash, and her chest presses against mine. It's only for an instant, but it's enough to make my pulse scoot up a notch.

Her glossy lips leave a sticky mark on my cheek that I don't want to wipe off. Her sleeve pulls up, revealing a colorful arm tattoo. It looks fully dry to me, which means some asshole did it for her when she was underage.

"Does your dad know you've got that tattoo?"

Lily rolls her eyes, and I don't blame her. I sound like a scolding father. But I feel as protective of her as if she was my own.

"I'm eighteen now, Jesse. I don't need Daddy's approval for everything I do. I'm a legal adult. I can make my own decisions. About everything."

She bites her lower lip, and her gaze travels down my body.

Am I imagining it, or is Lily flirting with me? There's no mistaking. She's making eyes at me. Which is all sorts of wrong. Especially because I *like* it.

"Is your aunt here?" I need to put some distance between us.

Lily opens the door wide while still standing against it, so that as I push past her, my arm brushes her chest.

Christ, the heat coming off her is enough to scorch my skin. What am I thinking? She's eighteen, and I'm forty-one. It's indecent. Not to mention the fact that she's Bruno's daughter, the club president, and my best friend. I can't be thinking these thoughts about her. Not if I want to keep my balls.

I move quickly through the dining room and into the backyard. I find Valerie with Gina and Kray running the BBQ. A few of the other club members are here, but mostly it's kids. Lily's school friends, I guess. They're lounging around the pool. A couple of them are drinking beers under Valerie's watch. And there's the distinct smell of weed. Sure, it's legal in this state, but I'm pretty sure Bruno wouldn't want drugs at his daughter's party.

I follow my nose and find a group of teenagers sitting around the pool. There's a guy perched on the edge of a lounge chair holding court. He's gesticulating wildly, grasping a doobie in one hand and a beer can in the other.

He goes to pass the joint, but I get there first, snatching it out of his hand.

"Hey man, what the fuck?"

I throw it into the pool, and it sizzles as it goes out.

"It's legal, man." The kid stands up, but when he sees me, he hesitates. I'm a big man, six foot three, broad shoulders with a solid frame, and I'm wearing the Underground Crows MC patch.

"Not in this house it isn't."

He wisely keeps his mouth shut and sinks back onto the lounger. I feel him scowling after me as I head across the yard and back to the adults.

Kray hands me a beer, and we chat for a while. He

introduces me to his old lady, Cleo, and their adopted daughter.

But I'm only half listening. I scan the yard until I catch sight of a flash of green. Lily's leaning against the fence, laughing at something a boy is saying to her.

A wave of jealousy rips through my body, and I curl my hands into fists. I want to go over there and pull him away from her. Which is ridiculous. What right do I have?

As if she knows I'm looking at her, Lily raises her gaze straight to mine. The boy is oblivious that he's lost her attention, droning on about something. Lily gives me a small smile. Time seems to slow down as we eye each other across the lawn.

Her cheeks dimple when she smiles. It suits her, and I wonder what she looks like without all the makeup on.

Valerie goes quiet, and I realize someone's asked me a question.

"Hmmm?"

I turn quickly back to the conversation as Kray hands me another beer. Sucking on it greedily, I will myself not to look at Lily. Instead, I focus on Valerie. We talk for a while about how she's getting on with Bruno's case. She thinks she'll have him out in a few months.

That's a relief to hear. The club needs a president, and Bruno is the best there is. I've known him since we were at school together. He's my best friend as well as the club president.

I excuse myself to use the bathroom and make my way into the house.

As I'm walking back down the hall, I hear raised voices in one of the bedrooms. A girl, protesting. I walk quietly to the door and look in. Lily is up against the wall and the man who was smoking the reefer has her pinned there, his arms on either side of her head.

"I'm not interested, Karl. You're high."

"Just a kiss, Lily."

He leans toward her and I lunge forward, grabbing him around the neck.

"She said no, fuck head."

The guy's eyes bulge out of their sockets, and his face goes red. I'm squeezing him too tight, but I don't care. My body's full of rage. I could kill this fucker for laying a hand on Lily.

"Jesse." Lily's voice is pleading, and her eyes are as wide as his. The last thing I want to do is scare her.

I release the kid, and he grabs at his throat. "What the fuck?"

I don't give him a chance to try to explain. Grabbing his shoulder, I turn him toward the door and march him out of the house. He stumbles through the front door, and I give him a good shove to make sure he's got the message.

"Get the fuck off this property and stay away from Lily."

He stumbles down the steps and out the gate, not looking back. I've scared the shit out of him, and I hope he has the good sense to stay the fuck away. Who's stupid enough to fuck with the President of the Underground Crows's daughter?

When I turn around Lily's watching me, her green eyes flashing dangerously.

"I had it under control, Jesse."

"Is that what you were doing, sweetheart?"

"Yes. I was about to knee him in the balls, actually."

A smile tugs at my lips. I don't doubt that for a second. She looks like she could handle herself, but I'd rather be there to protect her. I can't explain the wave of protectiveness that's come over me.

She bites her lower lip, and she looks up at me in a way that sets my skin on fire.

"Why would I let a boy touch me when I'm looking for a real man?"

My breath catches in my throat. There's no denying what she's implying. I take a step towards her, and she backs up. Now I'm the asshole backing her against the wall. But I make no move to step away.

"Careful, Lily…"

My eyes flicker to her lips, so full and glossy and kissable. I'm aching to kiss those lips, to pin her to the wall and show her what a real man feels like.

"I've been waiting for you to get back, Jesse."

She arches her back so her chest grazes mine,

sending a raw heat coursing through my veins. I'm confused by what she's saying, by this whole situation.

I've been around Lily ever since she was a baby. I bounced her on my knee and chased her around the clubhouse when she was a little girl. As she got older, she got shy around me. I thought she was just being an awkward adolescent girl and didn't pay her much mind. I've barely seen her in the last few years. With Bruno inside, she's not been around the clubhouse, and I've not thought much about the teenage girl.

"I'm a woman now, Jesse. I'm not a little girl anymore."

She steps towards me and presses her fingernails lightly on my chest. It's so delicate, her touch, but it sets my whole body zinging. My gaze follows her fingers as they trail down my stomach and stop at my naval.

"Lily. What are you doing?"

I should pull away but I'm enthralled by her, by the things she's making me feel. Waking up my senses and heating my blood.

Her lips part, and she leans toward me. I can smell her sweet breath and cherry lip balm. My head goes fuzzy, and I'm almost overwhelmed by desire.

"Daddy doesn't need to know."

Daddy...Bruno, the MC president. Shit.

I spin away from her just before her lips brush mine. There is no way in hell I should be here kissing

Lily. She's eighteen. She's the president's daughter. It cannot happen.

I throw open the front door and stumble down the steps, needing to put as much distance between us as possible.

"I gotta go," I call behind me.

When I get on my bike, my heart's beating fast. I almost kissed the president's daughter. My best friend's daughter. She's got a teenage infatuation with me, and I almost exploited that.

What the hell was I thinking?

1
JESSE

Four years later…

"Where the fuck is she?"

Bruno paces the clubhouse, his phone pressed to his ear, Lily's number on repeat. I'm just as anxious as he is. It's not like Lily to not show up when she's meant to.

We're heading off on a run this morning, and Bruno wants everyone to stay at the clubhouse as a precaution. We're still getting heat from The Reapers, and he's scared of retaliation. With most of the club gone, he wants the women and families kept safe.

Lily was supposed to meet us here for breakfast, but she hasn't shown up.

"Is she working today?" I ask, trying not to let him see how worried I am.

Lily works part time at the primary school down the road. She's getting work experience while she finishes her teaching degree.

It suits her, teaching. The tough talking rebel teenager has mellowed into a tough talking young woman. She's now more likely to wear soft dresses than tight jeans and less makeup too. She's still beautiful and still off limits.

Lily's never tried to kiss me again. But I've never given her the opportunity. At first I tried avoiding her, not trusting my feelings. I thought her teenage infatuation with me would pass. But she's a hard woman to stay away from. She lights up the room when she's in it, her green eyes twinkling with laughter. I can't keep my eyes off her when she's around, and I gravitate towards her. It's hard not to let my feeling show.

"Can you track her phone?"

Bruno looks at me like I'm crazy. "Of course I can track her phone."

He opens an app, swiping his fingers quickly until her finds her. "She's on Harlow Drive."

It's not where she lives, and I look as confused as Bruno. I don't know why she's there, but at least we have her location.

Bruno strides toward the door just as Lyle comes out of the office and cuts him off.

"Pres. We might have a problem."

Bruno runs his hands through his hair and glances at me. It's an important run, and people are relying on him.

"Jesse. I need you to go get Lily."

I'm not going on the run today. I'm one of the men staying behind with the families. I don't mind. It's an opportunity to hang out with Lily without her father hanging over us. We're always more relaxed together when Bruno's not around. We've never nearly kissed again, but we talk a lot, and I like making her laugh.

"Let me know that she's safe. And find out what the fuck's at Harlow Road."

Just then Gina comes out from the kitchen carrying a tray full of bacon sandwiches.

"Harlow Road? Isn't that where Lily's friend Matt lives?"

My head jerks around at the same time as Bruno's, and we both stare at Gina.

"Who the fuck is Matt?" I growl.

If Bruno wasn't so concerned, he might see the wave of jealousy that grips me, making my blood boil and my body shake.

"Are they dating?" Bruno's fists clench, a sobering reminder of what he'll do to anyone who dates his little girl.

Gina gives Bruno a look like he's stupid. "It's seven-thirty in the morning, and she's at his house. I'd say they're dating."

"If some kid's ravished my daughter…" Bruno turns away, unable to finish his sentence.

"She's twenty-two years old. You've got to let her go sometime, Bruno." Only Gina could get away with speaking to the Pres like that. She's like a sister to him, but even Gina can't talk sense into him this time. Bruno's furious, and so am I.

"Take her to the cottage, Jesse. I don't want her in town trying to sneak off to meet some guy. Stay with her until I get back."

I don't have to be told twice. I grab my keys and head out to my bike.

2
LILY

I take a sip of warm coffee, ignoring the buzzing phone on the kitchen counter.

Matt gives me a pointed look. "You gonna answer that, Lil?"

I keep both hands firmly clasped around the coffee cup and glance down at the phone. It's Dad, again. "No," I say firmly.

Matt narrows his eyes at me. We've been friends since the first day of college, and he knows me too well.

"You're up to something, Lily. I don't know what it is. But if it involves angering your dad, you know, the badass president of a biker gang, then I don't want to be a part of it."

I vaguely feel bad for dragging Matt into this, but it was the only way I could think of. "You're already a part of it, hon."

"I was afraid you were going to say that. He's not gonna turn up with all his biker friends and have some kind of shootout, is he?"

Matt looks more excited than worried. "You've been watching too much *Sons of Anarchy*. The Crows aren't like that. My dad's a good guy."

Matt presses his lips together and nods vigorously. "Mm-hmm, yep. A good guy who did three years inside."

"Dad was set up for that."

But I know how it looks. The club has gone legit in recent years, but they're not squeaky clean. I know what my father is. He works to his own moral code.

The buzzing of my phone finally stops, and in the silence that settles over the kitchen, Matt slides a bagel across the counter to me.

"I should have been suspicious when you wanted to come over and have an all-night Ryan Gosling film fest."

"What's wrong with having a movie night with my best friend?" I ask innocently.

Matt looks like he's going to question me further, so I quickly change the subject.

"You excited about the date?" Matt's met a new man, and he spent most of the night texting him. They're finally meeting in person tonight.

His face goes dreamy when he talks about Ethan.

"Yeah. Maybe this time he won't turn out to be an asshole."

Matt's had about as much luck with men as I have, but at least he puts himself out there, unlike me. There's only one man for me, but if I wait around for him to make a move, I'll be ninety before I lose my virginity.

The roar of a bike crashes through my thoughts and sends a nervous flutter into my stomach.

"Did he track your phone here?" Matt sounds nervous now.

I knew he would find me; I'm just surprised it's taken him this long. I peek through the blinds, and my gut clenches when I see that it's Jesse. My plan has worked better than I realized. But when I see the furious look on his face, I'm not so sure.

"Ooh, he's hot." Matt's peeking through the blinds next to me, oblivious to what I might have just unleashed.

"Um, Matt. You might want to wait upstairs."

"And miss all the fun?"

There's a loud thump on the door, and suddenly I'm wondering why I thought this was a good idea. I might be about to see my best friend get beat up.

"Please go upstairs."

But Matt's shaking his head, looking amused. "I think I know what you're up to, Lily."

I grab my bag and open the door, but before I can leave Jesse pushes past me and into the kitchen.

"Is this the shithead you spent the night with?"

Matt's eyes go wide as Jesse grasps him by the collar, but Jesse doesn't give him time to speak.

"Do you know who you're fucking around with? That's the Underground Crows's president's daughter."

"Jesse…" I try to calm him down, but I've never seen him so enraged. A vein throbs in his neck, and I think he's going to hit Matt. This is not what I meant to happen.

"Stop it."

It's lucky I'm a big girl, tall as well as wide, and I throw my weight around, managing to wedge myself between them and get Jesse's attention.

You can't just barge in here and manhandle my friend."

Jesse turns his gaze on me, and it's terrifying and hypnotic the way he devours me with one look.

"If he's laid one hand on you…I swear to God, I'll ring his neck."

This has gone way too far. I wanted to make Jesse jealous, to shock him into making a move on me, but I didn't imagine it would get so heated.

Matt's eyes are bulging in his head, and if he gets hurt it's all my fault.

"Stop it, Jesse."

He takes my concern for confirmation that there's something between us, and he pulls his fist back. I close my hand around it before he can strike.

"We were just watching movies, I swear."

"So you didn't sleep with him?" It comes out as a

growl. Jesse's like an enraged bull claiming its territory, and if I answer the wrong way, there's no doubt Matt will get hurt.

This is what you wanted, isn't it? I tell myself. But I didn't think it would go this far. I thought making Jesse jealous would finally get him to make a move. I don't want anyone getting hurt.

"No, I didn't sleep with him, not that it's any of your business. I'm still a virgin." My cheeks flush crimson at the admission. The reason I'm still a virgin is standing right in front of me, his eyes blazing with jealousy.

The vein in Jesse's neck pulses at my words, but the anger goes out of him. He lets out a sigh, and the tension falls from his body. He releases Matt, who slumps onto the counter rubbing his throat.

My arms go around Matt. "I'm so sorry."

"I'm fine, Lil." He's got a smile on his face, and I can tell by the way he looks at me that he's figured out what I'm up to.

"Get your bags, Lily."

I'm furious with Jesse. I know I bought this on myself, but I didn't expect him to come in here like an animal.

"I'm not going anywhere with you…" My words are cut off as Jesse picks me up and throws me over his shoulder.

I'm a big girl, but he lifts me up as if I'm light as a feather.

"Jesse. Put me down."

My fists pummel his back, and I blush red in embarrassment. This is not how it was meant to go.

Matt's smirking at me, thinking this whole thing is hilarious. "Have fun," he mouths and gives me a little finger wave before Jesse carries me out the door like a sack of potatoes.

3
JESSE

Lily's body pressed against me is a bad idea. My arm is around her legs, and the way she wiggles against me makes her pussy rub against my shoulder. If I wasn't so angry, I'd be hard as a rock.

I always knew the day would come when Lily met a man, and I knew it would be hard to take. What I wasn't expecting was the jealous rage that flared up inside me. This uncontrollable anger and need to let everyone know that she's mine.

Lily is mine.

I've tried to deny it. Ever since that day four years ago when she pressed up against me at her birthday party, I've wanted Lily. I've tried to ignore these feelings, to ignore the longing I have for her.

I've watched Lily grow from a rebellious teenager into a graceful young woman, and my feelings have grown with her. I've spent too long denying myself, and now some other man is going to claim her. She tells me that guy's just a friend, but how long until another guy comes along and I lose her forever?

"What are you doing, Jesse? I can walk just fine."

She bangs her fists against my back, but she's not struggling too hard. I wonder if she's enjoying this as much as I am. When I reach my bike, I slide her down in front of me.

Her green eyes flash, and she presses a finger to my chest.

"You could have hurt him."

I grab her finger in mine and pull her forward so her face is inches from mine. We're both breathing hard. I want to tell her how I feel, but I'm still too angry.

"But I didn't. Now get on the back of the bike. I'm taking you to the cottage."

I throw her bag into my saddle bag and give her my spare helmet. She doesn't speak to me. She's sulking, probably angry that Bruno sent me. But she does get on the bike. As we cruise down the highway, her arms go around my waist and her body leans against mine. It awakens all my senses. I've been wanting this for so long, and I almost let her slip through my fingers.

We take the winding roads heading up to the cottage. The club owns it, and it's tucked into the clifftop and concealed down a remote gravel road. Nobody knows it's here, and if any there's any heat from The Reapers, Lily will be safe. And I've got her all to myself for a few days.

"Get off the bike," I snap once we reach the cottage. Lily gives me a hurt look and I hate that I used that tone with her, but I'm still furious at myself.

The gravel crunches under our feet as I take her bag into the cottage and dump it in the main room.

"You can take the big room." She's followed behind me, and I almost bump into her as I turn to leave.

"Why are you so angry?"

She looks so hurt and confused, and I hate myself for doing that to her.

"You were supposed to meet Bruno this morning. He didn't know where you were." But I know that's not it. She knows it too. "Why didn't you meet him, Lily? That's not like you."

She looks away, biting her lower lip, and I wonder if there's something she's not telling me.

My eyes flicker to her lips, so round, so plump. She's got no makeup on at this time of the morning and her skin is flawless, her soft round cheeks tinged pink.

"Why are you so cross with me, Jesse?"

I put my hand on the wall so she's pinned against it. He chest heaves up and down with every breath. She looks at me expectantly, her eyes imploring.

"Because I thought you were with another man, and that thought almost destroyed me."

I've finally admitted what I've kept locked up all

these years. Her eyes go wide, and her breathing gets shallow.

"There's only ever been one man who I wanted Jesse." She grabs the edges of my jacket and pulls them, frustration creeping into her voice. "You, Jesse. It's only ever been you. Can't you see that?"

I see it all right, but I've denied it, not wanting it to be true. But I'm done with denying my feelings. If I don't make a move, I'll lose her to someone else.

"It's only ever been you for me too, Lily. This morning, I thought I'd waited too long…"

My fingers brush over soft lips.

"You're mine, Lily. I won't wait around for another man to claim you."

I press my mouth to hers and she parts her lips, letting me in, meeting me in the kiss. We've denied ourselves for too long, and now our bodies press together. My hands slide around her waist, feeling every curve of her and pulling her toward me. I want to consume her, devour her. I've waited so long for this.

My phone buzzes in my pocket, and I know without checking that it's Bruno. Everything sweet about the last few moments crashes around me as reality kicks in.

"Is that Dad?" Lily asks.

A wave of guilt sweeps over me as I answer the phone.

"Do you have her?"

"Yeah. We're at the cottage."

"Good." There's relief in his voice. He has no idea what I was about to do with his daughter.

"Keep her safe. I'm counting on you, Jesse."

He hangs up, and guilt weighs heavily on my shoulders.

Lily's the president's daughter, my best friend's daughter. Bruno's trusting me to look after her. I can't let him down, no matter how much I want Lily. What the hell was I thinking?

4

LILY

*J*esse keeps to himself for the rest of the morning. I hear him outside cutting wood for the fireplace, and I hate that after finally admitting his feelings he's still struggling to accept them.

I wanted to make him jealous today. I'm tired of waiting around for him to make a move. It's so obvious there's something between us. Whenever we're together, we talk easily. We laugh. I can't believe no one's noticed the connection between us.

I know he feels the same. I also know he'll never do anything about it out of respect for my father. And I respect that. But sometimes a girl has to go after what she wants. And what I want is Jesse.

I make us a simple pasta salad for lunch, and when Jesse comes to the table, there's a new awkwardness between us. We eat mostly in silence, and I hate this new tension between us. If felt like we were getting somewhere this morning, and now Jesse's back to denying his feelings.

He finishes his bowl of pasta and looks me squarely across the table. "Why didn't you come to the clubhouse this morning, Lily? You knew your dad was waiting for you."

I put my fork down slowly, stalling for time.

This is what I wanted, isn't it? When I hatched this plan? But now that the moment of truth is here, I feel afraid that maybe I've got it wrong.

"I didn't come to the clubhouse this morning, Jesse, because I knew Dad would track me to Matt's place."

Jesse's eyes narrow.

"Why would you want to worry your dad like that?"

He's looking at me intensely, and I think he already knows the answer.

"It's not him I did it for." My voice comes out as a whisper. "I did it for you, Jesse. I wanted to make you jealous."

He looks at me a long time.

"And how did that work out?" But he's not cross. He looks amused.

"I almost got my best friend beaten up." We laugh, and just like that the tension's gone from the air. We might be laughing together again, but I'm not going to let this opportunity slip through my fingers. Jesse might have too much respect for my dad, but it's not just up to him. It's time to make the first move again.

Scraping my chair back, I stand up and walk slowly around to Jesse's side of the table. My heart's hammering in my chest, but I have to do this. I can't wait any longer. Jesse wants me, but he'll never make the move out of respect of my father. But I'm not afraid of going after what I want.

"I know there's something between us, Jesse. You can't deny it. I've been waiting for you for the last four years. Longer. Ever since I was sixteen, I've wanted you. But you never noticed me. Dad's too overprotective. He thinks I'm a child, but I'm not. I can make my own decisions. I can be with who I want to be with. Dad's going to have to accept that."

My hand falls on Jesse's shoulder, and he tenses. My leg slides over his thighs until I'm straddling him. His breathing quickens, and I feel him instantly harden underneath me. A surge of wet heat floods my panties.

"Lily…" It comes out as a low growl, a warning, and I love the way my name sounds on his lips.

"I'm a woman now, Jesse. I want to experience everything a woman can experience."

"What are you doing, Lily?" His voice is choked, and I can see the struggle that's going on inside of him.

"I'm giving us a chance." I take a deep breath and look him dead in the eye. "I'm tired of waiting, Jesse. Either you take me now, or you don't take me at all."

5
JESSE

Lily's words hang in the air. Her thighs are wrapped around mine, and it feels too good having her on my lap.

There are so many reasons why I shouldn't be with her. She's twenty years younger than me. Her father is my best friend and the president of the club. But there are so many reasons why I should.

She grinds her hips into me, and her eyes are pleading.

"God, Lily, you're making this hard."

"It's not hard, Jesse. You either want me or you don't."

It's so simple for her, but she has to understand what it means, the implications.

"I'm not playing with you, Lily. Once I claim you, you're mine. Do you understand?"

Her eyes sparkle, and I think she's going to cry. "It's what I've always wanted."

"You've got to understand the risks. When Bruno finds out, I might be out of the club. I'll be exiled."

"I don't care," she says. "As long as I'm with you."

She slides my jacket off, her fingers trailing down my arms and over my biceps. I grab her around the waist and pull her onto my hips, grinding my hardness against her, letting her feel what she does to me.

"Be careful, Lily. You're playing with fire."

Her eyes flash. "Then let me burn."

Holy shit. This woman's too much. I'm powerless to resist. She grinds into me and I push upwards, needing to feel her. I kiss her slowly, tasting her neck and moving down her tender throat to her breasts, so full and so sweet and so perfect.

I grab her by the hips and lift her out of the chair. She wraps her thighs around me, and I carry her to the wall. Pressing her against the wall, I hold her in place as my hand pushes up her skirt. My finger trails over the gusset of her panties, and they're damp already.

"Jesse," she whines, and I love the way she says my name, all breathless. I pull the edge of her panties aside and slide my finger over her wet folds. She gasps and quivers under my touch.

"Are you really still a virgin, Lily?"

"Yes. I've been waiting for you."

Holy Christ. This woman's my undoing. More guilt

THE BIKER'S FORBIDDEN LOVE

wracks my body. I'll be taking something precious from her, deflowering Bruno's little girl.

She senses my hesitation and tilts her hips so her damp pussy grazes my fingers. Her hand takes mine, and she pushes it forward until the tip of my finger finds her opening.

"We shouldn't do this."

But it comes out feebly. There's no way I can stop now. Not with Lily writhing against the palm of my hand.

"Yes, Jesse. We can."

She moves forward so my finger sinks into her pussy. She cries out, her chest pushing forward, her tits sticking out.

"Fuuuck." She feels good. So tight. I can't imagine what my cock will feel like inside her.

"We shouldn't be doing this, Lily." I grab at her dress and tug hard. The buttons pop off, and her breasts tumble out and into my eager hand.

I press my mouth to her tits, sucking on her sweet, pillowy breasts, taking each nipple into my mouth and sucking hard as my finger works her pussy.

"Jesse!" she cries out, and I can feel she's close to coming undone.

Guilt wracks me, and I try to pull away. But Lily grabs my hand and holds it in place against her core.

"I need this, Jesse. I need you."

And when she says that, God help me, I start making circles with my palm pressing onto her hard nub, with her tit in my mouth and my cock hard as stone.

"Jesse…" She pants my name over and over until she screams it, her pussy tugging on my finger as the orgasm makes her body convulse.

I should stop now that I've given her what she needs, but my need for her outweighs any guilt I feel.

My hand pulls out, and I rip her panties right off. She fumbles with my belt buckle, releasing my cock. It's sticking straight up, and she gives a squeal when she sees it.

"We don't have to do this, Lily; we shouldn't do this."

But my cock's already circling her entrance, and she's got her head back, moaning. I'm torn between my need for her and doing the right thing. There's something about it being forbidden that makes it more thrilling. She senses it too, and every time I tell her we should stop she moans, a little high-pitched sound that drives me wild.

Instead of moving away, I hoist her leg up. I get a glimpse of her sweet slit, the opening glistening. My cock is ready and waiting, and she grabs it and guides it to her dripping entrance. We pause with the tip pulsing at her opening. Our eyes lock, and I'm powerless before her. The woman I love, wide open in front of me, finally mine to take.

"We shouldn't be doing this." The forbidden words make her shudder as I slide into her. "We shouldn't do

THE BIKER'S FORBIDDEN LOVE

this, Lily," I say as I sink my cock into her grasping pussy. She cries out, and her moans are almost my undoing.

Her pussy tightens around me and squeezes me like a vice. I feel her virgin barrier breaking around me, and knowing that I'm the first man claiming her breaks down my own internal barrier.

I grab her hips and I thrust deep, making her cry out. We shouldn't do this, but fuck that. She's my woman now. This is my pussy.

She's hot and open for me, and I fuck her hard against the wall, grabbing her hips and slamming myself into her. Thrusting deep until my balls slap against her asshole and she's screaming out my name, her nails digging into my shoulder as she comes. I slam home, my cum exploding deep inside of her, not caring that we haven't used protection. I want to breed her to tie her to me. To make her mine for good.

Everything I've been waiting for for the last four years, the built-up longing and want, everything I am, shoots out of me and into her waiting womb. Everything I have is now hers, my thick cum burying itself deep inside her pussy and tying her to me with a bond that can't be undone.

My breathing calms, and I pull Lily to me. My cock slides out of her, leaving thick ropes of cum trickling down her thigh.

"You're mine now, Lily." I take her cheeks in my hands and pull her face close to mine. "Whatever happens. There's no going back from this. I love you. And you're mine."

She smiles at me sleepily, and there's a look of triumph in her eyes. "It's what I wanted."

Lily set a trap for me, and I walked straight into it. And I'm happy to be caught.

6
LILY

I wake up to the smell of bacon and fresh coffee wafting through the house. I can hear Jesse humming to himself in the kitchen. He sounds happy, and that makes me happy. My body aches in a most delicious way and I stretch lazily, remembering every detail from last night.

After he took me roughly against the wall, we made love slowly in the bedroom. The second time was tender and slow, showing the real connection between us.

We fell asleep entwined in each other, and sometime in the night I awoke to Jesse's hardness pressing into my back. I was half asleep as he bent me over, tugging gently at my nipples, and fully awake by the time he plunged himself inside of me.

I lost count of the number of orgasms I had. My pussy feels tender, but in such a good way.

"Morning, beautiful."

Jesse's carrying a tray of food that barely covers his naked body.

"You always walk around naked?" Not that I'm complaining. It's obvious he works out. He's in great shape, with taut muscles and a perfect round butt.

"Only when it's just the two of us."

There's a stack of bacon on a plate with scrambled eggs, toast, and coffee. The smell makes my tummy rumble, and Jesse chuckles.

"I knew you'd be hungry after last night."

He sets the tray on the bedside table and leans over to give me a kiss. My fingers trace the lines of the dragon tattoo snaking up his left thigh.

His cock twitches at my touch, and I let my fingers continue lazily up his thigh.

"Lily…" Jesse lets out a warning growl. "You must be sore from last night, sweetheart. I need to give you a break."

It makes sense what he's saying. But I feel like a kid with a new toy at Christmas. I just want to play, especially when he parades around naked. My pussy might be tender, but it's already throbbing, and there's sticky heat between my legs.

"Don't you want to play?" I give him my best pout.

He shucks in his teeth as my fingernails scrape over his balls.

"As much as I'd like to get back in that bed and ravish you, you need to eat." He's trying to be firm with me, but his hard cock tells me how he really feels.

"I know something I can eat."

Before Jesse has time to protest, I scoot across on my knees and take his cock in my hand as I slide the tip into my mouth.

Jesse grunts in surprise, and I love that I can have that effect on him.

"Lily, what are you doing?"

I pop his cock out of my mouth and stare up at him, giving him my best wide-eyed look.

"I think I'm giving you a blowjob, but it's my first time, so…" With a smile on my lips, I take him in my mouth and suck hard.

"Jesus, Lily. That feels good."

I slide my lips down his cock while keeping my eyes on his. I see the moment that he gives into his need, the moment that he surrenders to me, and it feels like a victory. Everything about winning Jesse over feels like a victory. I've wanted him for so long, and I know why he resisted and I don't blame him, but there's no going back from this now.

His cock is huge in my mouth, taking up all the space, and I gag as I try to take all of him in. I use my lips and my hands as I work his shaft, tugging him into my mouth. It feels clumsy, and I catch his skin with my teeth, but Jesse doesn't seem to mind.

"Slow down, sweetheart. Use your tongue." He takes my head in his hands and guides me to a slower pace.

I love that he's instructing me and I do what he says, slurping my tongue around the base of his cock and then trailing it up his shaft like I'm licking a lollipop.

I look up at him as I'm doing it, and I'm pleased to see the heat in his eyes.

"Fuck, Lily. You keep doing that I'm gonna come right in your mouth."

"Good," I say, before plunging him deep inside my mouth again.

"Fuuuuck."

Jesse holds the back of my head and pushes me gently down his shaft. I gag as his cock hits the back of my mouth, but then I feel my throat open. This is amazing. I'm taking him all in. I can take him right to the back of my throat, and he loves it. It's uncomfortable, but so fucking sexy.

My pussy is dripping as I take Jesse's cock in and out of my mouth. I feel so sexy giving him pleasure, knowing that he's powerless, that I hold all the power right now.

My hand slides to the base of his cock, and I cup his balls. I literally have the man's balls in my hand. I fucking love it, but I need some release too. With my other hand, I move my fingers down my body till I get to my slick folds. I'm so wet and needy that as soon as I put pressure on myself, I feel an orgasm building.

My mouth moves faster over his cock, and I taste his salty precum. My very first taste of Jesse's cum, and it's so fucking sweet.

"Lily..." He groans as his fingers tangle in my hair, tugging at the roots and sending zings of sweet pain through my skull, adding to the sensations of the moment.

"I'm going to come."

He tries to pull my head off him but I suck tight, shaking my head. I want to taste him. He seems to get what I want, and again I feel the moment that he gives in to me.

"Fuuuck." He's grunting obscenities, and there's no gentleness now. He's got my head in his hands, and he's pounding me onto his cock as he fucks my mouth.

It's so hot, and I can't hold out any longer. My pussy convulses under my fingers, and I scream over his cock as I suck him hard. At that moment, I feel him explode into my mouth. Hot cum hits the back of my throat, thick ropes almost choking me while my orgasm wracks my body, shaking me to the very core. Jesse's shouting my name as I tug on his cock, sucking every last drop of him down.

My body stops shaking and I feel him go limp within me, completely spent. Sliding his cock out of my mouth, I wipe my sticky lips. Jesse pulls me up towards him, and we sink onto the bed. He kisses me deep and hard, and I love that he's tasting his own semen on my lips.

"Fuck, Lily. You make me come undone."

We hold each other close, my heart beating with his.

I've never felt this close to anyone in my life. This connection. This belonging.

"I love you, Lily," Jesse whispers into my neck. "This is forever, you know that, right? This isn't some weekend thing. I want you in my bed every night. I want to wake up with you every day."

My heart swells, because this is what I want too. "That's all I've ever wanted, Jesse."

He squeezes me tight, and in that moment, I've never felt such pure happiness.

7
JESSE

*T*he last two days have been the happiest of my life. No contest.

Hanging out with Lily is amazing She's the sweetest, funniest, and sexiest woman I've ever met. We've fallen into an easy routine: cooking together, watching old movies in the evening, and making love. In the shower, on the bed, against the wall, and up against a wooden gate when we went for a walk.

We've been at it so much that her pussy is tender, not that she'll admit it. I put my foot down this morning and said no sex today. It's hard to keep my hands of her, but I need to give my girl time to recover.

She's in the shower now while I'm in the kitchen making breakfast. This will be our last day at the cottage, and I want to make it memorable. Tonight I need to take her back to the clubhouse and face Bruno.

The guys will be coming back from the run tonight,

and the sooner I tell Bruno about us, the better. He won't take it well, but there's nothing I can do to stop this thing that's between me and Lily even if I wanted to. I always knew I was in love with Lily, but the last few days have shown me it's more than that. It's a once in a lifetime kind of love. The kind of love where you grip it with both hands and never let it go.

She's my soul mate. I know it. I'll fight for that if I have to.

There're bunches of yellow flowers that grow wild around the cottage, and I pick some while Lily's in the shower. I'm arranging them in a glass of water for her breakfast tray when the roar of a bike makes me scramble to the window.

Dust flies up behind the rider as he stops in front of the cottage and pulls his helmet of. It's Bruno.

"Fuck."

He must have come back early from the run. I'm not ready for this, and by the way he strides to the front door, I can tell he's not in a good mood. Foreboding tugs at my gut as I hurry to meet him.

"Where's Lily?" he asks immediately.

"She's fine. She's taking a shower."

His eyes dart around the living room at the remnants of our weekend together. Empty wine glasses on the coffee table, the open door to the bedroom behind me. I surreptitiously slide one of Lily's bras off the arm of the couch and let it drop to the floor.

"How did the run go?"

I'm stalling for time. Lily and I agreed that we'll tell Bruno together. If he sees how in love we are, it'll be easier to accept.

As Bruno tells me about the trouble he had with the run, I hear the water turn off in the shower. A few moments later, I sense movement behind me.

"I don't think I can go a whole day..." Lily's voice dies on her lips. She gasps as she sees her father and tries to cover her naked body.

"Cover yourself up, girl."

Bruno looks away quickly and tosses the throw from the couch at her as Lily retreats into the bedroom.

"What are you thinking?" he calls after her. "Coming out here like that?"

I know exactly what she was thinking, but I'm not going to tell her dad that.

Suspicion clouds his face, and he follows Lily into the bedroom we've been using. The blankets are all messed up on the double bed. A pair of Lily's panties are on the floor.

It's obvious we've both been sleeping in the one room.

"What the fuck is going on?"

This is not how I wanted to tell Bruno. He's like a bull when he's angry, charges first and asks questions later.

"I can explain."

His eyes dart to the crumbled pile of tissues on the bedside table and realization hits.

"Have you been fucking my daughter?"

I cringe at the crass language. He's technically right, but it's more than fucking. We've been making love, exploring our connection, forming a lifelong bond. But there's no way to dress this up for her father.

"I'm in love with Lily."

"What the fuck are you talking about?" It's like he doesn't even here me he's so blinded by rage. "You've been boning my girl?"

Bruno strides towards me with his fist in the air. I don't even duck, and the punch hits me on the side of the cheek, catching my ear. My vision blurs and it fucking hurts, but I deserved that.

Lily screams, but I barely hear her over the ringing in my ears.

"You're my best friend, Jesse. You're my best fucking friend."

The betrayal in Bruno's voice is more than I can bear. I get why he's angry, but he needs to understand what's going on between us.

"It's not like that, Bruno. I love her. I want to be with her."

"She's half your fucking age."

I try to raise my eyebrows, but my head hurts. Lily's the exact same age as Scarlett, Bruno's young wife. But Bruno's so angry I can't get a word in edgewise.

"How long has this been going on for?" Bruno demands.

"I've loved her for the last three years." His eyes go wide, and I realize my mistake.

"You've been fucking her for three years?"

"No, no, no…" I hold my hands up, but it's too late. Bruno comes at me, and this time I dodge the punch. He lunges forward, sending us both careening over the back of the couch.

His fist connects with my nose, and I taste blood. I think he's broken it and I might have lost a tooth, but I won't fight back.

"Stop it!" Lily screams at us, but Bruno doesn't hear or he doesn't notice. I'm not sure which.

"We're in love," I try to tell him, but he's not ready to hear that truth. All I can do is dodge his blows as best I can. I deserve this. I disrespected my best friend, and I deserve this beating. I won't fight back; I won't make it worse. If getting pummeled by Bruno is what I have to do to win Lily, then I'll gladly take the beating.

8
LILY

I scramble into my clothes as the shouting in the living room gets more intense. My dad just saw me naked, which is all kinds of embarrassing, but that's the least of my problems. If I don't intervene, he's going to really hurt Jesse.

"Stop it!" I scream, but no one's listening to me.

Dad's got his fists all over Jesse, and Jesse's not fighting back. I understand why he's not. He thinks he deserves this, but no one deserves to be beat up this way.

"Stop it!"

I try to get between them to make it stop. I'm a big girl, and I can throw my weight around. But when I try and pull them apart, Dad shoves me out of the way. It's not rough, but it's still a shock.

No one's listening to me, so I do the only thing I know of that will get Dad's attention.

Dad loves the people in his life fiercely, but his love for his bike is a close second. Grabbing his keys from the table, I dangle them in front of his face.

"If you don't stop right now, I'm gonna take your bike and crash it."

He gives me a sideways glance, but I can tell he doesn't think I mean it. I'm mad as hell at him. He's not giving us a chance to explain. No wonder Jesse waited so long to be with me. This is a side to Dad that I've never seen, and I don't like it.

Suddenly needing to be away from here, I race out of the house. I need to get away from this violence, away from this male energy that thinks everything can be solved with fists.

I jump on Dad's bike and don't bother with the helmet. The wheels kick up the gravel as I turn her around and speed off down the driveway.

I don't want to be around this, and if there's one thing that will get Dad's attention, it's taking off on his bike. I only hope that it stops the violence that's going on inside.

9
JESSE

My cheek stings, and there's the taste of blood in my mouth. I think my nose is broken, but I still don't fight back. I deserve this. Every hit is a reminder of the betrayal of my best friend. And every hit makes me more determined to be with Lily.

It's only the sound of a bike tearing up the gravel outside that stops Bruno's fists. The door's wide open, showing Lily on Bruno's bike snaking down the gravel drive and kicking dust up behind her.

"Shit." Bruno strides to the door, but she's already long gone. "She's not wearing a helmet."

"Lily can ride." I try to reassure him, but I don't feel crazy about it myself. Lily's been on a bike since she was a baby, but Bruno's bike is a beast, and I don't know how she'll handle the turns in the road.

"That woman is a handful, I swear to God…" Bruno sags against the doorframe, the fight going out of him.

If Lily's intention was to stop him from beating me up, then it worked. His anger has turned to concern, and it may be the opportunity I need to get through to him.

"I didn't mean to disrespect you, Bruno. I denied my feelings for three years. But we love each other."

He runs a hand through his hair, and I see the torment on his face, the father not wanting to let go.

"She's a child, Jesse. She's half your age."

"She's the same age as your wife."

He shoots me a dirty look, not happy that I'm bringing up Scarlett.

"This is different."

"Is it? How?"

"Because Lily's my daughter." Even as he says it, I can see he realizes how unreasonable it sounds.

"She's an adult, Bruno. A woman who can make her own decisions. I want to make her my old lady. I want to marry her. It's hard, I know, but you have to let her go."

He lets out a deep breath and gazes up the driveway. Lily's long gone, but the dust still hangs in the air.

"Is it what she wants?"

I think back to the last few days, how she made me jealous to get my attention. The good times we've been sharing, the promises we've been making to each other. I hope like hell she means them like I do.

"Yeah, I think so."

"Will you look after her and treat her right?"

He's questioning me now like a concerned father, and I feel hopeful that he's coming around to the idea. It feels weird having to explain my intentions to my best friend, but if it's what I have to do for Lily, then I will.

"I'm gonna buy a place somewhere for the both of us. She can finish her studies, work or not work, whatever she wants to do." I want to add that we'll start a family, but I don't want Bruno to be reminded of what that entails right now.

"You sure this is what she wants?"

"I haven't asked her formally yet. But if you give us your blessing, then I will."

Bruno paces the porch. I hope that showing him respect by asking for his daughter's hand will go a long way toward healing out friendship.

"And if I don't give you my blessing?"

I shrug my shoulders. "Then we'll be together anyway."

I hold his gaze so he gets my meaning. There is nothing in this world that will keep me and Lily apart. If it means leaving the club, if it means going to another state, that's exactly what we'll do to be together.

Bruno breaks eye contact and keeps pacing. He gives a soft chuckle that's tinged with sadness.

"I knew I'd have to hand her over to another man one day. I just thought I'd have more time."

Hope fills my heart; he's definitely coming around

to the idea. "You're not giving her away, Bruno. You'll still be in her life."

"I know." He shakes his head. "You'll understand if you have a daughter one day."

He puts his hand on my shoulder, and the pressure is a little bit harder than I'd like.

"You have my blessing, Jesse." I can't help the grin that spreads across my face. "But you break her heart, you fuck with her, you make my little girl cry, and I will rip your balls off one by one."

I don't doubt the man, but I have no intention of hurting Lily. Now all I want to do is find her.

"Can you trace her?"

Bruno pulls out his phone and brings up the tracking app. In a few minutes, I know exactly where Lily is. I quickly splash water on my wounds, then get on my bike.

It's time to claim my woman.

10
LILY

As soon as I get to the Pacific Highway, I find a place to stop. I'm not comfortable on Dad's bike, especially without a helmet. I can ride, but I'm not stupid.

There's an overlook on the side of the road, and I pull up there. A stack of large rocks forms a barrier to the cliff below, and I scramble up and take a seat. It's nice looking out at the ocean as cars whizz past behind me. It's calming after the violence at the cottage.

I was fuming when Dad turned up at the cottage. I didn't realize how angry he'd be when he found out about me and Jesse. I don't get it. I'm a grown woman. I can make my own decisions. No wonder Jesse denied his feelings for so long.

I couldn't watch them fighting like that, and I hope going off on Dad's bike will snap him out of it.

I don't have to wait long before a bike pulls up at

the overlook behind me. Jesse climbs up on the rocks to join me, and when I see his face, guilt overwhelms me. There's blood trickling from his nose, and his eye is already swollen.

"Jesse, we need to get you looked at."

I start to climb down, and he puts a hand out to stop me.

"It's fine, Lily. It looks worse than it is."

Jesse brushes off my concern and climbs up next to me on the rock.

"My dad's a brute. I can't believe he did this to you." There's a tissue in my pocket, and I blot it against the blood. "We need to get you to the clubhouse; get you patched up."

Jesse stops my hand. "Not yet, Lily."

There's something about the way he says it, the seriousness in his voice that gives me pause. He's spoken to Dad and agreed we can't be together. The last few days didn't mean the same to him as they did to me.

"What is it, Jesse?"

"It might be hard for you to understand, but I deserved that. Your dad and I have been friends for a long time. It was disrespectful to go behind his back."

Panic flutters in my chest. This isn't how this was meant to go. Dad was meant to give us his blessing, not scare Jesse off.

"But it's what I want. It's what we both want, isn't

it?" My voice goes up an octave, and Jesse rest his hand on mine.

"Relax." He smiles and then winces. He's hurting, and I hate that it's because of me.

"I've sorted it out with your father. We have his blessing."

I stare at Jesse, not daring to believe him. "Are you serious?"

"There's just one condition."

My heart sinks. This is where he says we have to wait for two years, or we can't date seriously.

"I can't wait, Jesse. I've waited too long."

He's smiling again, and I don't know what the joke is.

"I wanted to show your father how serious I am about you. But even if he didn't give us his blessing, I would have done this anyway."

I don't know what he's talking about, and not knowing makes me irritated.

"Get to the point."

You're so impatient." Jesse chuckles as he slides off the rock in front of me. "I didn't have time to pick up a ring. Lily, I've loved you since the day of your eighteenth birthday party. I tried to stay away from you, but this thing that's growing between us is beyond my control. We're meant to be together, Lily. I can feel it. Will you honor that connection and make me the happiest man alive? Will you marry me?"

My breath catches in my throat, and happy tears sting my eyes. It's more than I could have hoped for.

"Of course I'll marry you. Of course."

It's everything I ever wanted with the only man I've ever wanted. I don't care about the age gap between us or my father's disapproval. Jesse is the man I'm meant for.

I slide off the rocks, and he captures me in his arms. As our lips meet, I taste his blood and I know our love was hard won. But it's the right kind of love, the love that will last forever.

EPILOGUE

JESSE

Six years later...

*B*rightly colored balloons are tied to the backs of chairs, the juke box, and every damn thing I could attach them to. I used three bottles of helium to fill up this place with balloons. But it's worth it for my little girl's 5th birthday.

"Daddy, can I have a cupcake?"

Bella tugs on my leather jacket and looks up at me with big round eyes. They're the same green as her mother's and just as irresistible.

"Please Daddy..."

Lily and Gina spent hours arranging those cupcakes into a three tiered birthday cake. But I'm sure they won't miss one...

"Just one." I select a cupcake from the back of the display and hand it to my eager daughter. "Don't tell Mommy okay."

She nods solemnly and takes off with her treasure.

Lily will kill me if she knows I'm handing out cupcakes from the cake display. But it's Bella's birthday, and whatever my little girl wants, my little girl gets.

Bruno was right. Now that I have a daughter, I understand how he feels. I'll do anything to protect my little girl, and I don't even want to think about what will happen when the time comes to hand her over to another man. At the moment, I'm the main man in her life, and I want it to stay that way for as long as it can.

The other love of my life comes waddling through the door. Even at nine months pregnant, Lily still takes my breath away.

Pregnancy suits her and her wide frame handles it well, but at this late stage, she's red-faced and sweating. It doesn't help that she's got Ajax on her hip, wiggling around, full of energy now that he's just woken up from his nap.

I hurry to take our son off her, and his little hands cling to my neck.

Lily's been up too late planning this party, and even with help from the other woman, it's been exhausting for her. Gina and Valentine baked the cakes, Willow and Scarlett set up the room, and Cleo booked the entertainment. That's how it is here. Everyone helps each other out anyway they can.

"You need to sit down."

I pull out a chair for her, and she sinks into it gratefully, giving a sigh of relief. Lily slips her shoes off and rests them on another chair, wriggling her swollen ankles.

"I'm disgusting when I'm pregnant, aren't I?"

She looks forlorn. But to me, she's still the most beautiful woman in the world.

"Not at all."

I set Ajax down, and he toddles off to find the other children. "You're beautiful to me." I run my hand over her round belly and feel a kick. We stare at each other in wonder. It won't be long now until we meet our next child.

I love Lily when she's pregnant, and I try to breed her as often as I can. The new baby will make three, and I don't think we'll stop until we've got half a dozen, maybe more.

A gaggle of children run into the clubhouse, chasing each other around the room.

"Watch the table!" Lily calls as they race around the cupcake tower.

Gina's two wild boys lead the pack, followed by Lyle's oldest girl, her wild hair streaming behind her as blonde as her father's. A trail of younger kids chases after them trying to keep up.

There's a wail as one of the toddlers falls over, but Quinn scoops him up, tossing him into the air, and he's soon laughing at his daddy.

Bella comes running up to Lily, telltale chocolate smudged all over her face. Lily gives me a stern look.

"Did you give her a cupcake?"

I hold my hands up. "Guilty."

Lily laughs. She knows how much I dote on my little girl, on our whole family.

She wipes the chocolate off Bella's face, and the little girl scampers off. She heads straight to Bruno. He's got a child of his own on one hip, but he still scoops Bella up with no effort.

It took him a while to come around to the idea of me and Lily, but once he saw how much I loved her and how good we were together, he soon softened.

We bought ourselves a little house, and we're filling it with children and laughter. But our real home is here at the clubhouse, and this is our family.

A few years ago, we were all gruff, old, lonely bastards, but here we are with women and children. Even Pans seems happy, his arms wrapped protectively around Willow's pregnant belly.

It's amazing what love can do to a man. And when you get a bunch of hardass men falling in love together . . . wow, it could just about change the world.

Having a family changed things for me in the same way it did for Bruno. We got out of every illegal business deal that we had. Everything we do now is above board. We make our money in legitimate ways. We might not be as rich, but there are other ways for a man to be rich. And if you count your wealth in blessings, then I'm the wealthiest bastard around.

I've got my woman, my family, and my club. What else could a man want?

* * *

WHAT TO READ NEXT

PROTECTING HIS BRAT

This brat needs to be taught a lesson, and I'll be the one to discipline her...

Since retiring from the special forces, I've set up a team of elite personal security guards.

But I wasn't expecting the daughter of my first client to be such a brat.

Adrianna thinks she can play me, but she needs to be taught a lesson.

I'll be the one to take her over my knee.

She needs to learn that the only game I'm playing is for keeps.

Protecting His Brat is an OTT age-gap romance featuring an older military hero and a young curvy virgin.

Keep reading for an exclusive excerpt or visit:
mybook.to/ProtectingHisBrat

PROTECTING HIS BRAT

CHAPTER ONE

Bronn

It's an unusual house. Box-shaped rooms, jutting out at odd angles, looking like building blocks a child has stuck together.

The sun glints off the floor to ceiling windows, making me wince even behind my sunglasses.

It doesn't look homely, the hard lines making it look uncomfortable, unwelcoming, like a fortress. I should know. I've been staring at it all fucking day.

A black Mercedes waits on the driveway, the chauffeur as bored as I am.

But I'm good at waiting. I learned it in the Army, how to be still while remaining alert and how to spring into action when needed.

All good traits to be a security guard, which is about

the only work I could find when I retired from the special forces.

Still, clients pay top dollar for ex-military, especially when you've been in the Green Berets.

Finally, the front door opens, and my client, Phillip Brooks, steps out.

His dark tailored suit contrasts with the sun gleaming off the white walls of the house. His wife stands in the doorway, twisting her hands nervously, looking at him with doleful eyes.

He slides an arm around her waist, and I look away as he embraces her. I feel a pang of regret. The military life never allowed me to settle down with a woman. I wonder what it's like to have someone to say goodbye to, someone to miss you when you're away.

He steps away, and she tugs on his sleeve, not wanting him to leave. Gently, he pries her hand off his arm and hurries down the stairs.

He stops next to me, and I get a whiff of bourbon and expensive aftershave.

"Don't let her leave the property."

I nod, letting him know I've understood his instructions.

My client explained the threat to me, the death threats he's been getting, his concern for his wife.

If someone had threatened my woman, I wouldn't be fucking off and leaving her alone. But it's not for me to judge. From what I understand, when you're in the oil business, like my client is, threats are a part of life.

The chauffeur holds the door open for my client, and he slides into the waiting car.

There's a wrought iron gate at the entrance to the property, and I scan the area around it, making sure there's nothing suspect before we open the gates.

As the car circles around the drive, I catch movement on the road.

My skin prickles, and I'm instantly on high alert. A black car is driving slowly down the road, too slow to be going straight past.

I jog in front of the Merc, holding my hand out to stop them. My client ducks down in the back seat, protecting himself from whatever threat this might be.

The black car comes to a stop outside the gate. It's got tinted windows, so I can't see who's inside.

Every fiber of my body is alert, my blood thumping, ready to meet the threat. I pull my piece and aim it at the car, keeping my hand steady.

The back door of the car opens, and I train my gun on whatever's going to come out of there. I won't be the first to fire, but if someone attacks, I won't hesitate to shoot.

There's the flutter of bright fabric, a flash of tanned leg, and a young woman slides out of the backseat. She's wearing a short, floaty dress that comes halfway up her thick thighs. It dips at the front, displaying a full cleavage of soft breast.

My mouth waters, and there's a twitch in my pants.

If this is how my clients' enemies attack, then I'm screwed.

She can't be a day over twenty, but my dick doesn't seem to mind the age gap.

The woman shuts the door behind her and saunters over to the gate.

She slides her large designer glasses down her nose and peers at me over the rim, unimpressed by the gun I've got pointed at her.

"If this is the welcome I get, I would have stayed away." Her voice is as pouty as her look. Sassy and sharp.

I've been trained to encounter all kinds of enemies but not an entitled brat with a sticky pink pout and a mane of golden hair clasping an overnight bag to her plus-sized chest.

A car door slams behind me.

"Put the gun down, Bronn."

I slowly lower my piece, but I can't tear my eyes away from the woman. She wraps both hands around the iron bars and leans forward rattling the gate.

"Open the gate, Daddy."

Her voice is whiny and petulant, like an overgrown toddler. Like a spoiled brat who needs some discipline.

My client strides forward, irritation in his voice. "You're supposed to be at college."

The woman tears one hand off the gate and swipes at her golden hair. "It was boring."

"Did you get kicked out?" My client's voice is clipped, his anger not quite disguised.

The woman gives him a sweet smile.

"I wanted to be here with you instead."

My client harumphs and pushes the code for the gate. It swings open, and the woman sashays through.

"I've got a business trip. You can stay here with your mother."

"Oh, great," mutters the woman, and even though I can't see behind her glasses, I'm sure she's rolling her eyes. If any kid of mine spoke about my wife like that, I'd tan their hide. But her father doesn't react.

"Don't give your mother any trouble," he barks at her. "I'll be back in ten days. You stay inside these gates and I'll deal with you when I get back."

The daughter does a slow twirl as if checking out her surroundings. Her eyes rest on me, and my body tenses as she looks me up and down.

"Who's the heavy?" she asks her father as if I'm not there.

"I'm Bronn."

Both the woman and her father look at me in surprise. To them, I'm the hired help, the silent security guard. But this brat needs to learn some respect. If her father isn't teaching her ,then I will.

She slides the sunglasses onto her head, showing off her large brown eyes. There's a mischievous look in them as she saunters toward me.

"Hello, Bronn."

My cock lengthens despite myself. I shift uncomfortably, clasping my hands in front of my body, hiding what's going on in my pants.

"I'm Adrianna."

From a distance, she was beautiful, but up close, she takes my breath away. I literally can't breathe as I stare at her, transfixed by her dark, playful eyes.

Heat sweeps over me, and I feel unbalanced. A surge of protectiveness rushes through me, and one thought bangs into my brain.

Mine.

"Bronn's here to protect you and your mother. Do exactly as he says and don't do anything stupid."

She's so close to me I can smell her cherry-flavored lip balm and expensive floral soap.

"Oh. I'll do exactly what you tell me to do," she murmurs so only I can hear.

My gaze flicks to her lips, so full, so pouty—just the right size for my cock.

Then she flicks her hair and flounces up the driveway.

I am so fucked.

To keep reading visit:
mybook.to/ProtectingHisBrat

GET YOUR FREE BOOK

Sign up to the Sadie King mailing list for a FREE book!

You'll be the first to hear about exclusive offers, bonus content and all the news from Sadie King.

> To claim your free book visit:
> www.authorsadieking.com/free

BOOKS BY SADIE KING

Sunset Coast

Underground Crows MC

Sunset Security

Men of the Sea

The Thief's Lover

The Henchman's Obsession

The Hitman's Redemption

Maple Springs

Men of Maple Mountain

All the Single Dads

Candy's Café

Small Town Sisters

Kings County

Kings of Fire

King's Cops

For a full list of titles check out the Sadie King website

www.authorsadieking.com

ABOUT THE AUTHOR

Sadie King is a USA Today Best Selling Author of short instalove romance.

She lives in New Zealand with her ex-military husband and raucous young son.

When she's not writing she loves catching waves with her son, running along the beach, and good wine, preferably drunk with a book in hand.

Keep in touch when you sign up for her newsletter. You'll even snag yourself a free short romance! www.authorsadieking.com/free